D1308690

BODY SAFETY ZONES

BSZ

WRITTEN BY
Ms. Terri Johnson

ILLUSTRATIONS BY
Mr. Ravon Holmes

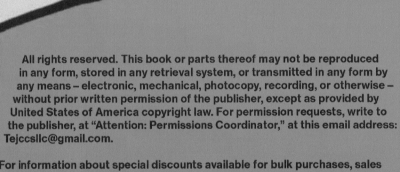

For information about special discounts available for bulk purchases, sales promotions, fund-raising and educational needs, contact Terri E. Johnson Clinical Consultative Services, LLC at tejccsllc@gmail.com or **www.persistenceistheway.com**

Body Safety Zones (BSZ) © 2020 by Terri Johnson.
Published by Terri E. Johnson, Clinical Consultative Services, LLC, Baltimore, MD 21215.

Editor: Ms. Catherine Orange, Baltimore, MD.
Illustration: Mr. Ravon Holmes, Baltimore, MD.

First Edition, 2020.
Hardcover ISBN: 978-1-7348377-1-1
Library of Congress Control Number: 2020906472

BODY SAFETY ZONES

BSZ

EST. 1920

RHODA LEE JONES ELEMENTARY SCHOOL

Prayer+Therapy
+Protecting your Energy
=Psychological Freedom
TJisms

RHODA LEE JONES

January- 20   November- 1

1906   1984

WRITTEN BY
Ms. Terri Johnson

ILLUSTRATIONS BY
Mr. RAVON HOLMES

This book belongs to:

_____

BODY SAFETY ZONES

"It is easier to build strong children than to repair broken men."

-Frederick Douglass

Dedication

This book is dedicated to all the children in my personal life, to my Baltimore City Public "school babies" and Mrs. Marlene O'Para (retired Educational Specialist for Baltimore City Public School Social Workers) for giving me a chance- the honor to serve and work as a School Social Worker. She hired me in August 1996!

Praise for Body Safety Zones (BSZ)

"Ms. Johnson has a plethora of educational and professional experiences, but more importantly she has a loving heart and a caring spirit. She wants nothing but the BEST for all the people with whom she interacts. She exemplifies what it means to care with open arms and an open mind. This book is just one example to demonstrate just how much she cares and her desire to show…Knowledge is Safety."

C.B. Orange, Editor, Retired Baltimore City Public School Teacher of more than 40 years.

"As a black male therapist who is a father, and also works with sex offenders in Baltimore City I am very excited that a book like this exists! As a father, I saw that this was a perfect ice breaker that I can introduce to my kids to talk about sensitive subjects such as appropriate vs. Inappropriate touching.

As a sex addiction therapist, I think this is a perfect book he helps kids advocate for themselves in case they themselves are victims are could be potential victims of sexual assault. Often times, victims don't realize that they are being groomed for sexual encounters. The victim can have completely innocent-sounding interactions with other people but not realize the danger they are in. This book breakthroughs that unawareness that sets the victim up to be a target. this book also provides vocabulary and safe visuals for children to understand what is and what is not appropriate.

If prevention is worth more than the cure then this book is a must-read for any parent, teacher, and school system wanting to empower and protect our children."

Jamaal Simmons, LMSW Black Male therapist, Father of two children, Sexual Addiction Therapist at the National Institute for the Study, Prevention, and Treatment of Sexual Trauma.

"What an awesome idea! Thank you for putting together this resource for children to educate them in a way they can easily remember. This is such an important topic. You have created a tool for parents and teachers to use to help many children for many years to come. You not only have a big heart but your passion to help people shines through your warm smile and gentle spirit. Thank you for shining your light in this world."

Dr. Susan Lee, Pediatrician and Partner of Howard County Pediatrics

"Body Safe Zones (BSZ) is a wonderfully energetic and fun read. As a father of three, I think it is very important that children are knowledgeable about their bodies and who and when they are allowed to be touched. I was especially excited to see this done in the right voice and tone for the children reading. This is exemplary of how Terri addresses everyone and why she is so good at working with kids. I think this is a book every child should read".

Howard C. Perkins III, M.Ed. Special Education Instructional Coach, D.C. Public Schools/ Author

Foreword

Youthhood is the premiere time to be unbounded, limitless, and prized. I can strictly remember thinking, "There is nothing that I cannot do", and "can't" was not a word allowed in my mother's house. I knew that if she continued to love me, everything would be okay. It did not take long to understand that I could receive love from others, too, and while nothing could mimic one as deep and true as her own, the very concept of receiving that love left a tremendous impression on my memory. How do we know what love is, and who is our teacher? To many, these answers stem from our childhood experiences; we gained most of our primary education from family and friends, who conditioned us into believing what is normal and even acceptable. In my own childhood, I was lucky to have another teacher and mother in my life, Terri Johnson, who taught me to know a very important difference.

Ms. Terri or Mama Terri, as I like to call her, often spoke to me about the importance of knowing what these acceptable forms of love looked like and who I should not take them from, and I can always remember her wise words, during countless encounters with danger, even today, in my adulthood. I met her at the age of four after just having moved into a new neighborhood. At that time, I was experiencing the divorce of my parents and separation from the only father figure I knew. This created newfound vulnerabilities. She quickly adopted me as her own child and facilitated a supportive and informative environment, where asking questions was encouraged and learning was an absolute must. Prior to her education, the only messages I can remember receiving to this day are "Stranger Danger" and "Don't take candy from strangers", both of which never formed much of a practical understanding as a naïve and impressionable little girl. My own personal experiences point to the purpose and need for young children to adopt the messages presented in this book. It is the primary education babies should have to ensure a safe life that is absent of irreconcilable traumas and full of timeless awareness.

~De'Ara Graves, Georgetown University,
School of Nursing and Health Studies Class of 2021

Welcome, friends, to Mrs. Rhoda Lee Jones Elementary School and to Ms. B. Persistent's wellness and awareness class.

Today, friends, we will start with getting our wiggles out by dancing, so we will be great listeners during Storytime! What is your favorite song to get all your wiggles out?

Great job friends! Now, let's put on our thinking helmets, click it on tight, turn our bionic ears up, up, upppp, zip and lock our lips, zippppp!

What are the different body safety zones? Oh my, wonderful, I see so-o-o many friends raising their hands to share the answers: Mimi, Pernell, Ty-Ty, Bar Bar, Shay Shay, Nakai'yah, Tyi'dre, and Dawn Dawn!

Ok, Mimi tell us what Body Safety Zone 1 or BSZ 1 is. Mimi said, "It's our mouth and only food, liquids like water or juice, snacks or medication should go in our mouths, Ms. B. Persistent."

"But, but, but Ms. B. Persistent," exclaimed Bar Bar excitedly. "We have special rules about medication, right?"

Excellent! Yes, Bar Bar, you're correct only certain people have permission to give you or other friends medication, so that you remain safe.

How about Bar Bar and Pernell, tell all of us who may give you and other friends medication?!

"Only our parents or someone our parents give permission, like our family members or friends may give us medication. Or dentist!" said Pernell. Bar Bar added, "Don't forget doctors, nurses or the workers on ambulances!"

"Correct!!! People who work on ambulances or ambos are called paramedics or emergency medical technicians, EMTs for short," said Ms. B. Persistent.

BODY SAFETY ZONES

Ok, what are the other Body Safety Zones that still need to be named? Shay Shay raised her hand and stated, "For girls, it's our top front, our chest. Body Safety Zone 2!"

Dawn Dawn called out, "Wait, boys have a top front, too! Can anyone touch them there if they want to because they're not girls?!"

"Wow, Dawn Dawn, I am so pleased to see you're really using your thinking helmet!!!" said Ms. B. Persistent.

REMEMBER, all of your body belongs to you, and if someone is in your space or touches you and you don't feel comfortable, you have a right to tell them!! Especially, tell a trusted adult RIGHT AWAY if someone touches your Body Safety Zones!

Ok, friends, let's go over the last two body safety zones 3 and 4 together! Our front (BSZ 3) and back (BSZ 4) bottoms are our private parts!

No one should touch you there unless you need help washing up or have had an accident in the bathroom. Only the person that takes care of you or has your parents' permission should help you.

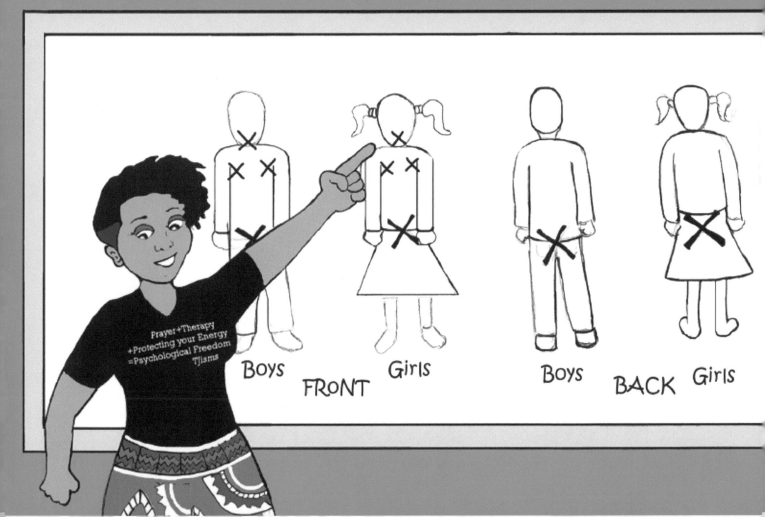

No one should take or ask you to take pictures of your Body Safety Zones. No pictures should be sent to anyone or put on social media because it is on the internet, FOREVER!

"MY BODY BELONGS TO ME! YOU DON'T HAVE PERMISSION TO TOUCH ME!!"

Prayer+Therapy
+Protecting your Energy
=Psychological Freedom
TJisms

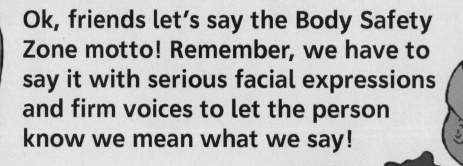

Ok, friends let's say the Body Safety Zone motto! Remember, we have to say it with serious facial expressions and firm voices to let the person know we mean what we say!

Put both thumbs up and point towards your shoulders as you repeat after me, "My body belongs to me! You DON'T HAVE PERMISSION to touch me!!"

Sometimes, a person who touches children will tell them lies or things that are not true such as, "You will get in trouble and locked up; I will hurt someone you love or your pet; I will not be your friend or love you anymore. This is a secret, so don't tell anyone!"

Don't trust them, friends. Tell a trusted adult such as the person who takes care of you, your parents, aunties, uncles, grandparents, sister or brother, call 911 for the police, tell your classroom teacher, trusted adult, school social worker, psychologist or counselor.

It can be someone in your family, parents, a friend, or someone you know in your community or school. But remember, <u>NO ONE</u> has the right or permission to touch your Body Safety Zones!

Acknowledgements

First, I have to thank God, for giving me courage, patience and guts to, finally, birth this labor of love and see it through to completion after so many years of apprehension, due to F.E.A.R!

To my crew of 2, Love Nuggets 1 & 2, my children: Jameela Alexander aka Mimi and Jabari Adeleye aka Bar Bar thank you for giving me a reason to be my true self, to live, to know love deeper than I ever thought was possible and forgiving me for my many imperfections. I'm not capable of expressing, in words, how much you both mean to me and for God to bless me with two "Masterpieces." I'm forever grateful!

To my nieces and nephews: Pernell Baylor, Tyshaun aka Ty Ty and Tyshana Price aka Shay Shay, Nakai'yah and Tyi'dre Martin. I have never considered any of you as my nieces and nephews but my children, it was a goal of my heart for all of you to be more like siblings than cousins, and for the most part you are! I love every one of you and pray nightly for your health and happiness. Love, Auntie

Play niece: Dawn Lucas aka Dawn Dawn, Auntie TJ is so proud of how intelligent, caring and brave you are, and I enjoy our sleepovers. Thank you for loving me!!!

Gift daughter: De'Ara Graves, I'm so proud of you and love you as if I gave birth to you. You are an amazing, young woman who I know will contribute dramatically and positively to the public health/welfare of our community.

Willie Farmer: We have been through so much as individuals and as a couple! Thank you for loving me! God and laughter keep us going and with time, I pray you share your unbelievable TESTimony because I know it will save lives.

Sisters: Stacey, Tiera and Tishawna, my blood sisters, how can I express my love for the three of you? To my oldest sister, Stacey Johnson, you're a silent fighter, and I admire your strength more than you'll ever know. To Tiera Wilson-Martin my "big little sister," you have come a long way, and with God, you're unstoppable, keep P.U.S.Hing. I cannot wait to witness the many Mighty things God does in your life!

To my "baby sister", Tishawna Wilson-Hill: I'm so proud of your grit and gusto for your career and especially when it comes to your family (Danny and the kids). Continue to reach for your dreams, and when you get there go further, you can do it! Sisters, I love you, and you can't do anything about it!

Sister friends: Lynise N. Creek-I miss you so much, but I'm forever indebted to you for ALWAYS pushing me to go as far as I could with my education and business (your love continues to keep me pushing)!

Michelle: My personal cheerleader, encourager who gives it to me straight along with God's word, thanks for being such a loving friend throughout the years.

Kim: You're such a kind, patient, God-fearing, dedicated family woman, community stakeholder and a friend who inspires me.

To my friend, Elaine Morgan Sinclair: We go way back to 1990 and what adventures we had in our youth! Love DJ

Surrogate Mamas/Aunties: Mrs. Catharine Orange, Soror Loretta Bond, Mrs. A. Hyman, Margo Woodward-Barnett and Dr. Sonja-Egblomasse all of you have impacted my life, one since I was 19 years old, or the lives of my children. You are educators or clinicians who I admire and continue to aspire to achieve your level of sophistication, patience, and self-womanhood; you have truly enriched my life and my work as a social worker!

Ravon Holmes: Thank you, for your talented artistry and creating my vision!

Many thanks to the following Indie authors, for your words of advice, wisdom and encouragement: Bobby M. Holmes, Howard C. Perkins, III, Angela Brown Alexander, Ashley Stallings, Ty Allen Jackson, Floyd Stokes, Charlie Mills, Courtney B. Dunlap, Donnie Hill and Darryl Silver!!

To my Pumphrey Family and Support System: Thank you for giving me a strong and healthy foundation: Aunt Petie, Aunt Sibbie, Aunt Annie, Cousins: Bina, Tony, Evie, Bernie, Corn, Tia, Lisa, Reese, Kendice, Mark, Ronnie and Jarryn, A special thanks to the Revell family for allowing me to come to your house everyday sometimes even when you weren't at home! Thanks to: the Hines, Gibson, and Creek families, Mr. Houston, the fellas down "Watergate" and countless others who served as impeccable role models. My life was truly enriched during my primary years, in that enchanted community, as a little rug rat running around wild, fast and free!

East Baltimore crew: Mr. Randy, Ms. Francis, Lamont, Marc, Troy, Ringgold and many others who encouraged me to "get out and get going because you're a 'good girl'." I choose to keep the positives and the REAL education about life from Ensor St., Bond and Preston St., Dallas and Lafayette St., Gorsch and Harford, etc.

My Mamas, Mrs. Rhoda Lee Jones and Mrs. Minnie Horshaw Smith: Growing up, I always had strong women around me and was blessed to hear information straight up without chasers! Mrs. Minnie Horshaw Smith (my gift grandmother) and Rhoda Lee Jones (paternal great grandmother) shaped my life in so many ways; it is impossible to share in this acknowledgement, but one thing that they both loved, other than their families, children. Both raised or took care of other people's children and provided loving and safe havens to youth in their time of need. Both are in Heaven now, and I thank them often for loving me and hope they're proud of my work with young people.

To my biological mother, Sharon A. Ford: Thank you for never giving up, despite unbelievable and unknown pain. Thank you for my life and the lives of my two younger sisters. I've been told too many times that I have a mouth like you, and I've come to appreciate it, in my later years. I'm so proud of you for facing your pain and living your life to the fullest. God made you like the automobile company; and Tiera often remarks, "Ford, tough!" I love you, Mommy.

RHODA LEE JONES

Glossary

911- is an emergency telephone number for the North American Numbering Plan (NANP) for police, ambulance or fire department.

Ambulance or ambo- a vehicle equipped for transporting the injured or sick.

Body Safety Zones (BSZ) Advocate- A person who pleads, maintains, defends, supports or promotes the interests of children right to protect their Body Safety Zones (BSZ).

Body Safety Zones (BSZ) Ambassador- A person who acts as a representative, promoter or teacher of the Body Safety Zones to children, so they will be protected and safe.

Body Safety Zones (BSZ) Motto- "My body belongs to me! You DON'T HAVE PERMISSION to touch me!!"

Body Safety Zones- four areas of the body that are private and should not be touched or entered by anyone. Zone 1-the mouth, Zone 2-the chest or breast, Zone 3- the vagina or penis and Zone 4- the buttock or gluteus maximus muscle and anus.

Child Protective Services (CPS)- is a specific social service provided by DHS to assist children believed to be neglected or abused by parents or other adults having permanent or temporary care or custody, or parental responsibility.

Community- a group of people with a common characteristic or interest living together within a larger society.

Emergency Medical Technician (EMT)- specially trained medical technician certified to provide basic emergency services (such as cardiopulmonary resuscitation) before and during transportation to a hospital.

Firm- strongly felt and unlikely to change.

Lie- to make an untrue statement.

Motto- a short sentence or phrase chosen as encapsulating the beliefs or ideals guiding an individual, family, or institution.

Permission- the act of permitting or consenting.

Persistent- the quality that allows someone to continue doing something or trying to do something even though it is difficult or opposed by other people. the state of occurring or existing beyond the usual, expected, or normal time.

Private parts (please use correct names)- vagina, penis and anus (this is a part of the buttocks).

Rights- something to which one has a just claim.

School Counselor- works in primary (elementary and middle) schools and/or secondary schools to provide academic, career, college access/affordability/ admission, and social-emotional competencies to all students through a school counseling program.

School Psychologist- is a type of psychologist that works within the educational system to help children with emotional, social, and academic issues.

School Social Worker- specialized in the field of practice devoted to school-age children and families in an educational host environment. Concerns addressed by school social workers include advocacy, attendance, bullying, need for community resources, coordinating homebound education, homelessness, home visits, suicidality, special populations, students with disabilities, and any other issues that may impede or inhibit students' academic success.

Truth- a fact or belief that is accepted as true.

Resources

Baltimore Child Abuse Center:
https://www.bcaci.org/ 410-396-6147

Childhelp National Child Abuse Hotline:
www.childhelphotline.org 1.800.422.4453

Children's Defense Fund:
https://www.childrensdefense.org

ECPAT: https://www.ecpat.org/

FBI/Help End Child Prostitution:
1-800-CALL-FBI (225-5324)

International Centere:
https://www.icmec.org/

International Society for Prevention
of Child Abuse & Neglect (World Regional Networks):
https://www.ispcan.org/ispcan-regions/

International Society for Prevention
of Child Abuse and Neglect: https://www.ispcan.org/

Male Survivors Trust:
http://malesurvivorstrust.org.uk/index.htm

Maryland Sex Offender:
http://www.dpscs.state.md.us/sorSearch/search.do

National Alliance on Mental Illness:
https://www.nami.org/

National Alliance on Mental Illness Maryland:
http://www.namimd.org/

National Center for Missing and Exploited Children:
http://www.missingkids.com/home

National Child Sexual Abuse Helpline
Darkness to Light: 1.866.For.Light or Text LIGHT to 741741

National Children's Advocacy Center:
https://www.nationalcac.org/

National Coalition to Prevent Child
Sexual Abuse and Exploitation:
http://www.preventtogether.org/

National Human Trafficking Hotline: 1-888-373-7888

National Parent Helpline:
https://www.nationalparenthelpline.org/find-support
(directory of various resources specifically to support parents) 1.855.427.2736

National Sexual Violence Resource Center:
https://www.nsvrc.org/

Office on Trafficking in Persons:
https://www.acf.hhs.gov/otip/victim-assistance

Office for Victims of Crime:
https://ovc.ncjrs.gov/humantrafficking/

PANdora's Box: https://pandys.org/

Parent Annoymous: http://parentsanonymous.org/

Polaris: https://polarisproject.org/

Psychology Today therapist directory:
https://www.psychologytoday.com/us/therapists

RAINN:
https://www.rainn.org/types-sexual-violence

Shared Hope International:
https://sharedhope.org/

Stop the Silence (Maryland):
https://stopthesilence.org/

Stop It Now!:
https://www.stopitnow.org/ohc-content/resources-for-parents-of-survivors

Stop it Now! UK and Ireland:
https://www.stopitnow.org.uk/

The Lucy Faithful Foundation:
https://www.lucyfaithfull.org.uk/
Confidential Helpline: 0808 1000 900

The NSPCC: https://www.nspcc.org.uk/
Helpline: 0808 800 5000 (concerned citizens) or 0800 1111 (18 under)

Therapy for Black Girls:
https://www.therapyforblackgirls.com/gd_therapist/

U.S. Department of Health & Human Services:
https://www.hhs.gov/programs/index.html

U.S. Department of Justice National Sex Offender Public Website:
https://www.nsopw.gov/

Violent Crimes Against Children:
https://www.fbi.gov/investigate/violent-crime/cac

Author's Biography

Ms. Terri Johnson has over 20 years of experience as a licensed (clinical) social worker, working in education, correctional facilities, Baltimore City Health Department, hospitals and managed care settings. Ms. T. Johnson, as she's lovingly called by her students, has been in private practice since 2009 and serves African American women, transitioning adults and various couples.

Ms. Johnson is a proud graduate of Morgan State University where she received a Bachelor's in Social Work and received a Master's in Social Work from the University of MD, School of Social Work, Baltimore.

The author of Body Safety Zones (BSZ) has spent more than twenty years working with young people making sure that they understand how special they are and how important it is for them to know how to protect themselves from people who would physically and/or sexually abuse or exploit them.

She enjoys singing, dancing, reading, coloring, creating and spending time with her two young adult children, Jameela and Jabari, and her pets: Bubbles (cat), Zoe Lee (Yorkie), and Hickory (turtle). She loves to volunteer cuddling NICU babies and driving the elderly.

"Our children are our greatest treasure. They are our future. Those who abuse them tear at the fabric of our society and weaken our nation. History will judge us by the difference we make in the everyday lives of children."

-Tata Nelson Mandela

CPSIA information can be obtained
at www.ICGtesting.com
Printed in the USA
LVHW070348071120
670965LV00010B/3